A Girl, Frank Burnside and Haile Selassie won first prize in Writing Magazine's "Life-changing" short story competition in 2016.

A Girl, Frank Burnside and Haile Selassie

Story by Steve Laker

Illustrations by Lola Laker

All rights reserved

© Steve Laker and Lola Laker

ISBN 978-1-542-61793-2

"Everything can change, suddenly and forever..."
Paul Auster

This is a story for when life changes...

Wishes don't usually come true. I've learned that by wishing for lots of things, only for those things not to happen.

Everyone wishes for things. That didn't work for me, so I wish for *not* things. When I wish for not things and things don't happen, that's wishes coming true.

My name is Ellie.

Frank Burnside calls me Sparks. Frank Burnside is my dog. I've had him since he was a puppy.

I wish I didn't have to grow up. I like being young. Frank Burnside says that I might soon lose things, like my ability to hold a conversation with a dog.

I wish that some things would go away, or not happen at all. For example, if someone I don't like is talking to me and I wish for them to go away, eventually they do and a wish comes true.

But how do you know if your wish has come true if you wish for something not to happen? How can you wish for nothing?

If I wish that my house won't burn down and my house doesn't burn down, does that mean that my wish has come true? If I wish that my dad doesn't get any more sad, is that another wish granted?

So, I don't wish for good things to happen but I wish

for bad things not to happen. It doesn't always work out. Not all of my wishes are granted.

They say the more you wish for something, the more likely it is to happen. You really have to want it and to will it from inside you with everything you have. You have to want something so badly that you're prepared to give up everything else for that one thing. It has to be the most important thing to you.

They say that you have to be good for your wishes to be granted. I try to be kind and good but maybe I'm not quite good enough.

Dad used to say it's like faith. He said that if you believe in

God, then God will guide you. He said that if you pray for something hard enough, your prayers will be answered. I don't believe in God because of all the bad things which go on in the world and because of what happened with mum and dad.

I used to pray that all of the bad things would go away but they didn't. Maybe I was asking too much.

So I tried praying for little things, like new clothes and toys but I didn't get them.

Perhaps God only has so many things to go around. Maybe he can only answer a certain number of prayers. So I stopped believing and gave up praying, so that other people might have their prayers answered.

I can't replace mum. I don't know how to tell dad that things will get better. I know they will but he wouldn't believe a kid. I want to tell him that I know what he's thinking and that I wish mum would come back too. I want to tell him that I know they only argued because of me. I know this because it's all that

I remember them doing.

I don't have many friends. When I do go out, I go for long walks with Frank Burnside: He's my best friend. That might sound strange because Frank Burnside is a dog but he understands me. We've grown up together.

Frank Burnside likes to walk.

He walks a lot. He talks too, but only to me. It's interesting to get a dog's view on things and Frank Burnside is a wise old dog.

You may think that when a dog barks at the TV, it's simply because they can bark at the TV. But dogs have their reasons. Sometimes they'd rather just watch something else.

With Frank Burnside it's horses. Frank Burnside says that he doesn't like horses because they're snobs. Horses just think they're better than dogs. But they're not. Horses can't talk for starters. They can't read either.

Frank Burnside told me that Marley, the family cat, goes by the name of Haile Selassie when he's entertaining friends in the kitchen: Mostly they smoke and play cards.

Postmen: It's not that dogs have anything against them, nor that they dislike the uniform. Dogs know that most of what arrives in the mail is advertising and bills. Dogs know this because they read their owners' post at night and they don't like what they see. It's true because Frank Burnside told me.

Sometimes Frank Burnside

will answer a question before I've even asked it. He knows what I'm thinking. It happened today, as I wondered what might become of me:

"Sparks, I'll have to go soon."

"Why, Frank Burnside? Where are you going?"

"To a wonderful place. Grown ups may tell you about it and you might not believe them but I can tell you that they will be telling you the truth. You see, soon we won't be able to talk Sparks."

"But I don't want us to stop talking Frank Burnside."

"Sparks, you're growing up. As you grow, things change. You will change and you won't be able to hear me any more but I'll always be beside you."

"But where are you going and why do you have to go, Frank

Burnside?"

"To a retirement home. Because I'm getting old."

"But you're not old Frank Burnside."

"I'm as old as you are Sparks but I've had a busy life and I'm tired. I've done almost everything I want to do. I've watched over you as you grew and now you are entering the next stage of life. Mine is over. You will live long after me. I can't look after you so well. I have a life to live after this one, in a different place, and so do you. There are different things to do there. There are many adventures to be had. When these old legs give up on me, I'll get new ones where I'm going. I'll be able to run and jump, faster and higher than ever. I'll be able to chase things and fetch things. I can't wait Sparks."

"I can, Frank Burnside. I don't want you to go."

"But I have to. I have one thing left on my bucket list and that's to stop you beating yourself up and blaming yourself for everything: Stop hurting yourself Ellie."

"It was the cat."

"Well, keep that cat under control when I'm gone. Do you want me to tell you where I'm going? I have to whisper as I don't want everyone to know."

Frank Burnside nuzzled up to me and whispered in my ear. He told me things which I must not write down: About where he was going and what would happen to me.

I'm not afraid any more. Frank Burnside has told me where he's going. It's where he longs to be and I'm not going to stop him because I love Frank Burnside so much that I just want him to be happy, even if I can't be with him. The place where Frank

Burnside is going really does exist because Frank Burnside said so.

I wanted to rush home and tell dad. I stood up and Frank Burnside looked up at me. "Let's run" he said.

"Why, Frank Burnside?" I said.

"Because one day we won't be able to."

And for that reason alone, Frank Burnside and me ran all the way home.

We were both panting for breath as we walked through the front door. I ran to my dad to tell him what Frank Burnside had told me. But dad was asleep. So Frank Burnside suggested I write everything down in this book. I wish it might help someone.

Frank Burnside is gone now. Thanks to him I can read back on what I wrote, way back when.

Thanks to Frank Burnside, I will never forget. My life was being changed by nature but Frank Burnside changed the way I saw things. He taught me that it really is possible to be gone and not forgotten.

I know he's still around. Haile Selassie is too.

For Jake
and
For Louis

The author has a website: www.stevelaker.net

Printed in Great Britain
by Amazon